The Ice Cream

Totally Fizzbombed

Julie Bertagna has had remarkable success in her short writing career. *Soundtrack* won the SAC's Children's Book Award and *Dolphin Boy* was shortlisted for the NASEN and Blue Peter Awards. *Exodus*, the launch title for Young Picador and her first novel for Macmillan, was shortlisted for the Whitbread Children's Book of the Year and won the Lancashire Children's Book of the Year and *The Opposite of Chocolate* was shortlisted for the Booktrust Teenage Fiction Prize.

She lives in Glasgow with her family and Flopsey the rabbit. *The Ice-Cream Machine* has been developed into a popular children's television series.

Visit Julie Bertagna's website at:
www.juliebertagna.com

D0257075

y share a studio near the Arsenal ground with Sue, and Arnie the dog.

Other books by Julie Bertagna

THE ICE-CREAM MACHINE

For older readers

THE OPPOSITE OF CHOCOLATE
EXODUS
SOUNDTRACK
THE SPARK GAP

The Ice-Cream Machine

Totally Fizzbombed

MACARONI 2

Julie Bertagna

Illustrated by Chambers and Dorsey

MACMILLAN CHILDREN'S BOOKS

First published 2005 by Macmillan Children's Books
A division of Macmillan Publishers Limited
20 New Wharf Road, London N1 9RR
Basingstoke and Oxford
www.panmacmillan.com

Associated companies throughout the world

ISBN-13: 978-0-330-43403-4
ISBN-10: 0-330-43403-9

5 7 9 8 6 4

A CIP catalogue record for this book is available from
the British Library.

Printed and bound in Great Britain by Mackays of Chatham plc, Kent

For Antonio and Cristina

Contents

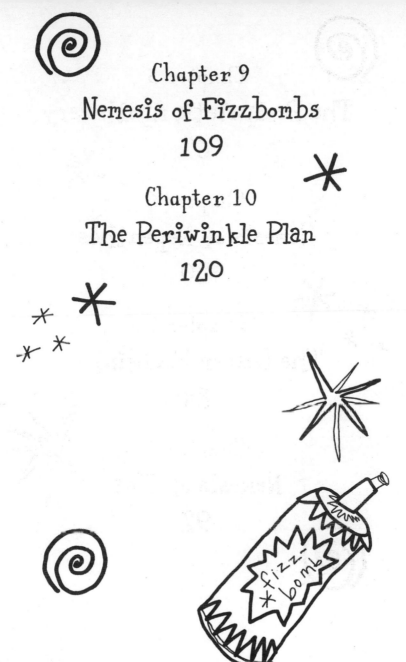

fizz-
*bomb

Chapter 1
Macaroni Goes Missing

Friday was the best day of the week.

It wasn't just because school was over and it was the start of the weekend. Fridays were best because, straight after school, twins Wendy and Wayne went to visit two very special friends. They were rather unusual friends too because one was an ice-cream van and the other was a goat.

They were no ordinary ice-cream van and goat. Wendy and Wayne knew that Macaroni, the ice-cream van, and Gina, the goat, were the most extraordinary ice-cream van and goat they were ever likely to meet.

Macaroni and Gina used to live with them but, after one too many adventures, they now lived in a quiet corner of a field on a farm at the edge of the village.

'Did you remember to bring the paint?' Wendy asked her brother.

Wayne nodded and drummed his heels on a large pot of paint that sat on the floor of the car.

'Good,' said Wendy, who had a paintbrush in each hand.

Last Friday had been wet and miserable. Sleety raindrops were plopping on to Gina's nose from a rusty crack in the ice-cream van's roof. The goat would jump every time a drop hit her nose but she wouldn't move. She was just too lazy, said Dad. He had suggested that they give the van a good, thick coat of paint before winter set in.

Dad revved the car up the hill to the farm.

'There's a mop in the boot in case Macaroni's flooded out,' he said. 'I'll try to mend the worst of the rust spots. Now, here we are.'

Wendy and Wayne jumped out of the car and climbed over the gate into the field.

'Oh,' said Wendy.

'Where is she?' said Wayne.

The twins stared at the spot where Macaroni usually sat. They could see tyre marks and a faded patch of grass where the ice-cream van should be, but there was no other sign of her.

There were only a few goats munching grass at the other side of the field.

'Can you see Gina?' asked Wendy, peering at them.

'She'd be over by now if she was there,' said Wayne, studying the goats. 'She knows we always bring her a treat.'

There was a clunk and a clatter as Dad threw the paint pot and mop over the gate, then clambered over after them.

'Well, thanks for leaving me to carry all the—' Dad stopped and stared around. 'Where on earth . . . ?'

'She's gone,' wailed Wendy. 'They've both gone!'

'Now, now, don't get upset.' But Dad stared in bewilderment at the empty field. 'Maybe

the farmer has moved them to another field. Ice-cream vans can't just drive off by themselv—'

Dad stopped. All of a sudden, he looked worried.

'Yes, they *can*,' sighed Wendy.

'If they're magical,' Wayne murmured.

'Don't be silly,' said Dad, pretending to be unconcerned. 'Isn't that Gina among those goats up there on the hillside?'

Wendy and Wayne shook their heads.

'Let's not jump to conclusions,' said Dad. 'You two wait here. I'll check with the farmer.'

He began to trudge up the hill towards the farmhouse.

Wendy and Wayne watched him, unable to think what to do. Mum and Dad *would* keep telling themselves that Macaroni was just an *ordinary* ice-cream van, despite having seen for themselves that she was quite *extraordinary*. Why were their parents so reluctant to believe in Macaroni's magic, even when it happened right under their noses?

'Um, Wendy,' said Wayne.

'Yes?'

'There was something I forgot to tell you.'

Wendy put her hands on her hips and frowned at him. Her brother sounded worried.

'We-ell, it might be nothing, but if they're gone it *might* be something . . .'

'*What?*' said Wendy.

'It's just that the last time we were here, Macaroni played a different tune.'

Wendy's frown deepened as she tried to remember. 'I never heard. Why didn't you tell me?'

'It was just as we were leaving. I was hungry,' said Wayne. 'I was thinking about pizza, so I forgot. It didn't seem very important then. But now I don't know.'

'She *never* plays a different tune,' said Wendy. 'It's *always* "Yankee Doodle".'

'Exactly,' said Wayne.

'Well, what was the tune?' Wendy asked him.

'I don't know,' said Wayne. 'She was playing it really softly. I thought she sounded sad.'

'And you never said a thing!' exclaimed Wendy. 'Anyway, even if you did know the tune, it's not going to help us find them.'

'Suppose not,' said Wayne, as Dad and the farmer appeared at the top of the hill, running towards them.

'What I don't understand,' said the farmer, scratching his ear in bewilderment, 'is how they stole a great big ice-cream van without opening the gate. I've got the only key and that lock hasn't been touched.'

'Who?' said Wendy. 'Who stole her?'

'I don't know, do I?' the farmer retorted. 'But somebody stole her, didn't they? Ice-cream vans can't jump over fences and take off by themselves, can they?'

Dad gave Wayne and Wendy a very hard look.

'Of course not,' said Wayne.

'Very odd,' said the farmer. 'Well, I'll go and phone the police – but I'll be surprised if we see that van again. It's probably being sold by some criminal gang as we speak.'

'But who would want a rusted, broken-down old ice-cream van that's full of goat and chicken droppings?' Dad asked.

'And what about Gina?' said Wendy.

'Some people will steal anything,' said the farmer. 'And some poor fools will buy anything.' He gave Dad a withering look. 'After all, *you* bought that van, didn't you? And that pest of a goat.'

'Ah, well, yes, but the van was in a lot better shape then, and anyway it wasn't me, it was my wife, and *she* bought the goat too,' responded Dad, but the farmer was trudging back up to the farmhouse.

'What do you think?' said Wayne, once they were back in the car. 'Has Macaroni gone off on her own or been stolen by a criminal gang?'

'I haven't a clue,' sighed Wendy. 'But a locked gate wouldn't stop a magical ice-cream van. Maybe you *should* try to remember that tune,' she told her brother.

'What good will that do?' said Wayne.

'I don't know,' shrugged Wendy. 'But it's the only clue we've got.'

Before they drove off, Dad turned around to look at the two children in the back.

'Now listen, I don't want you two saying anything to the police or anyone else about Macaroni being magic. It's all right if we as a

family – I mean, you two children – believe that, but I don't want people thinking your Mum and I are bonkers.'

Wendy and Wayne nodded, but when Dad had turned his back they looked at each other and grinned. Mum and Dad *were* bonkers. But they liked them that way.

'Oh, *no*!' said Mum when they told her Macaroni and Gina had gone missing. 'But she seemed happy at the farm, didn't she?'

'Wayne's not sure about that,' said Wendy.

'The farmer says they've probably been stolen by a gang of criminals,' said Wayne, who was now feeling exceedingly guilty about ignoring Macaroni's sad tune.

'Oh!' said Mum. 'I thought you meant Macaroni had run off somewhere.'

Dad gave her a stern look. 'Now, Elaine, we've talked about this. Macaroni is just an ice-cream van. She does *not* have any special powers.'

'Of course,' Mum agreed. 'Absolutely right. So you don't think that's why this criminal gang has stolen her?'

'What do you mean?' asked Wendy.

'Well, if anybody suspected that Macaroni *was* magi— I mean, unusual in some way, even though –' Mum caught Dad's eye – 'as your dad quite rightly reminded me, that's just plain silly. But if anybody *was* silly enough to think that, maybe they *would* want to steal her? It's just a thought.'

'Hmmm,' said Dad.

'A certain kind of person might see a certain kind of ice-cream van as a wonderful money-making opportunity,' added Mum.

'Hmmm.'

'If someone's stolen Macaroni we need to find her and rescue her – Gina too,' said Wayne.

'Hmmm – and how could we do that?' asked Dad. 'We don't even know if someone *has* stolen here. Maybe she's just taken herself off for a while, as your mum said.'

'Ah!' exclaimed Mum. 'So you *do* believe she's magic?'

Dad's face flushed with annoyance. 'I never said that. I just, um . . .'

'Ha!' said Mum, as Dad stuttered to an embarrassed halt.

Wendy and Wayne winked at each other. Their parents believed in Macaroni's magic after all!

'We could go out and look,' ventured Wendy. 'Couldn't we?'

'Where would we start?' asked Mum.

'The seaside,' said Wayne thoughtfully. 'Wendy, I've just remembered a bit of that tune. Macaroni was playing a different tune the last time we saw her,' Wayne explained to his parents. 'She sounded kind of sad.'

'And she's never played another tune in all the time we've known her,' added Wendy.

'That's true,' said Mum. 'What was the tune, Wayne?'

'I couldn't remember at first, but now it's

coming back to me a bit. It made me think of summertime. Oh, how did it go? Dumdee-deedee-dumdee – oh, what was it again?' he muttered. 'Dumdee-*dum*-dumdee-dumdee-dumdee-dum-dum,' Wayne sang out. 'Something like that.'

'Oh, I *do* like to be beside the seaside,' Mum sang back, in the very same tune.

'The seaside!' said Wendy. 'Maybe Macaroni has run off there again. That's where she went last time.'

'Last time?' said Mum and Dad together.

Wayne grimaced at his twin.

'Oops,' said Wendy.

'Something you want to tell us, you two?' asked Dad.

'We didn't want to worry you. It happened back in the summer – you see, Macaroni ran away with us to the seaside,' Wendy confessed in a rush, then looked warily at her parents. 'In the middle of the night.'

'In the middle of the—' Mum's mouth dropped open.

'*Night!*' said Dad, outraged. 'On your own?'

'Er, Gina was there,' said Wendy, as if that made it better.

'That's worse,' said Dad.

'Macaroni was homesick for the sea,' explained Wayne. 'We could tell. She was a seaside ice-cream van once, we're sure.'

'She brought us back safely,' Wendy reminded them. 'Don't be angry.'

'I'm not angry, I'm . . . I'm . . .' Mum looked stunned.

'Well, I am!' Dad exploded. 'And if that

ever happens again, you two will be grounded for the entirety of your childhood. Is that understood?'

'Yes,' said the twins meekly.

'Right then,' said Dad. 'If that's settled, we'd better go.'

'Go? Where?' said Mum, who still looked aghast at the thought of her two children driving off to the seaside in the middle of the night in the care of an ice-cream van and a goat.

'To the seaside, I suppose,' said Dad.

Chapter 2
On the Macaroni Trail

'*O*oh, it's not really a day for the seaside, is it?' Mum shivered as they stepped out of the car into a blast of cold sea air.

Apart from two large white dogs running along the sand, the beach was empty, as you might expect it to be on a bitterly cold November afternoon. The murky daylight was already beginning to dim and the air seemed foggy. But the fogginess was actually clouds of sand whipped up by the wind and swirled all across the shore and the seafront.

'I can't see anything. My eyes are full of sand,' cried Wayne.

'Mine too,' wailed Wendy.

'There's no sign of them out here,' said Dad, quickly scanning the empty seafront. 'Let's look in the town. We'll be sheltered in the streets.'

They hurried into the narrow streets of the seaside town, relieved to be out of the stinging, sand-sharp wind. They walked along thin pavements in single file, past a grocery shop, a shoe shop, a newsagent's, a curtain shop, a hardware store, a flower shop and a sweet shop, pausing at every corner to look along each street.

'They're not here,' said Wayne at last.

'Come on then,' said Mum. 'Back to the car.'

But Wendy stood staring at the quaint old sweet shop. Its dusty window was bright with coloured fairy lights and fat glass jars filled with all kinds of sweets.

'Pear drops, lemon barley twists, toffee bonbons, liquorice swirls, raspberry sherbet drops,' murmured Wendy, reading the names on the labels.

'It's too near dinnertime for sweets, Wendy,' said Mum.

'Can't I buy some for later? Look, Mum, it's an old-fashioned sweet shop. Like they were when you were a girl.'

 'Exactly how old do you think I am?' laughed Mum. 'A hundred?'

'You look good for your age,' quipped Dad. He peered into the shop.

From floor to cciling it was stacked with shelves of glass sweetie jars. There must be a hundred different kinds of sweets, thought Wendy.

'I never knew these old shops still existed,' said Dad. He looked as mesmerized as Wendy. 'I wonder if they have

any hot cinnamon gumballs. My granny used to buy me those when I was a boy. They really warmed you up on cold days like this.'

'Can I go in and see? Just for a minute?' pleaded Wendy.

'We're supposed to be looking for Macaroni and Gina,' said a very grumpy-looking Wayne. He always turned grumpy when he was cold, tired or hungry. Right now, he was all three.

'Well, I don't see any sign of them, do you?' snapped Wendy for exactly the same reasons. The old-fashioned sweet shop had taken her mind off her grumbling tummy.

'I can smell fish and chips,' said Mum, sniffing the air. 'That's what we need to warm us up. Then we may as well go home. This is a wild goose chase.'

'I agree,' said Dad. He began sniffing too.

A man walked past and an irresistible waft of salt and vinegar made their mouths water.

'Over there!' Wayne pointed to a shop from

which people were bringing out steamy,
paper-wrapped bundles.

Wayne made a rush for the fish-and-chip
shop, followed by his parents. None of them

noticed that Wendy gave a small gasp and stayed at the window of the sweet shop. All of a sudden she had a very intent look on her face, as if she was puzzling over which kind of sweets to choose – except she wasn't thinking about sweets at all.

'Here she is!' called Wayne. 'Hey, Wendy, stop ogling those sweets and eat your fish 'n' chips. They're scrummy.'

Wendy looked at her brother as if she was in a daze. Wayne thrust a hot, steamy bundle into her hands and she unwrapped the paper slowly, not ripping it open as she normally would. She gazed up at the sign above the sweet shop.

Sweet Ps

said the quaint, old-fashioned writing.

'What is it?' asked Wayne. 'Why've you got that dippy look on your face?'

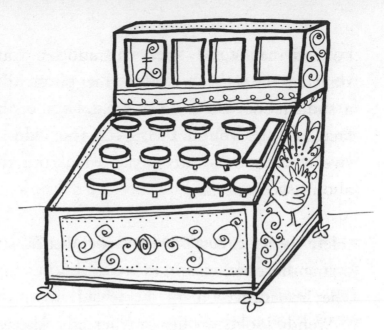

'That old money till on the sweet shop counter – it's so strange,' said Wendy, slowly munching on a chip.

'The till?' Wayne looked at his sister as if she'd lost her marbles.

'Remember Macaroni's peacock till?' said Wendy. 'Look, isn't it just like the one in the sweet shop?'

Wayne shrugged. 'So what?'

'Oh, never mind,' sighed Wendy.

'Come on, kids,' said Dad. 'Let's call it a

day. We can come back for another look when the weather's better. I'll phone the farmer and the police when we get home, and see if they've found them. It's too cold to wander the streets. Anyway, if Macaroni and Gina were around, I'm sure we'd know by now.'

The twins nodded. Dad was right. If they were in the area, *everyone* would know.

As Dad drove out of the seaside town, he wound down his window to clear the glass of fish-and-chip steam.

'Can hardly see a thing,' he said, wiping the front windscreen with his sleeve as they came towards a junction in the road. 'Oops, someone's had a bump.'

A man, a woman and a young girl sat in a red car, looking dazed. The bonnet was dented where they had bumped into the signpost on the traffic island that sat in the middle of the junction. A policeman, who was talking to the people in the bashed car, raised his hand to

halt Dad. Then he came over to them.

'Have you by any chance spotted a van, sir? A very brightly coloured van.' The policeman looked at his notebook. 'Possibly an ice-cream van. Though I must say,' he muttered, 'anyone who thinks they'll sell ice cream on an evening like this must be quite mad.'

Dad stared at the policeman. 'Well, as a matter of fact, we're looking for exactly that kind of van.'

'I'm sorry, sir?' The policeman looked confused. 'No, *I'm* looking for the van. Have *you* seen it?'

'No, but we're *looking*—' Dad spluttered to a stop as (Wayne and Wendy could see, quite clearly, from the back seat) Mum dug her elbow into his ribs.

'What's the problem, officer? How can we help?' Mum smiled sweetly at the policeman.

'Well, madam, as you can see, these people have had a nasty bump. They *say* it was caused by the antics of the brightly coloured van I described, which was, they *think*, being driven dangerously by a . . . by a . . . ahem!' The policeman glanced uncertainly at the family in the bashed car. 'By a *goat*.'

'A goat!' cried Wendy and Wayne.

'*Quiet!*' Mum hissed. 'Oh my goodness!' she said to the policeman. 'How strange. Are they sure?'

The policeman turned to the people in the bashed red car. 'Are you *sure*, madam? That it was a goat? You did say the van was going very fast.'

The woman got out of the car. Rubbing her
head, she came over to the policeman. Her
plump cheeks were angry pink. 'Officer,' she

said, 'do I *look* like the kind of person who doesn't know a *goat* when she sees one?'

'Not at all, madam,' said the policeman. 'But you did say you bumped your head when the accident occurred. Perhaps madam is a little confused about—'

'Jasper!' the woman called over her shoulder to a timid-looking man in the passenger seat. 'Come out here and tell this police officer that I am *never* confused. I am *entirely* in my right mind.'

'Well, he might have a point, dear,' suggested Jasper as he emerged from the car. 'You've had a shock. Perhaps you are the *tiniest* bit confused?'

'Jasper! I know what I saw. You saw it too.'

'I saw the van, Eleanor, dear. No one could miss that. But I can't say I saw a goat.'

The policeman scribbled in his notebook. He turned back to Wendy and Wayne's parents.

'You haven't seen a goat in the

neighbourhood, sir? Madam? Children?'

'No,' said Mum and Dad. Wayne and Wendy shook their heads.

'So the only person who saw a goat driving a van has banged her head,' muttered the policeman, scribbling hard. 'And therefore may be confused about events.'

'This is an outrage!' The woman's plump cheeks deepened from pink to purple. She was so angry that they wobbled when she spoke. 'I know what's what, officer, and I tell you I saw a goat driving an ice-cream van *perilously* across that junction!'

'Now, now, Eleanor,' said Jasper, looking embarrassed. He took his wife's arm. 'Do let's keep calm, dear.'

'Don't "*now, now*" me.' Eleanor shook off Jasper's hand and glared at the policeman. 'Officer, I expect you to pull out all the stops to find that van. What is the world coming to? Goats driving vans – without a licence, I'll bet – and nothing done to stop it, while

innocent drivers are *ridiculed* by the police. Meanwhile, that maniac goat and van are still on the loose!'

Wendy looked across at the girl in the back seat of the bumped car. She looked around her own age. As Wendy wondered if the

accident had given her a bad fright, the girl
suddenly stuck out her tongue.

I hope she *did* get a fright, thought Wendy,
and she stuck out her own tongue at the girl.
The policeman caught her eye and she pulled
her tongue back in.

Wayne wound down his window. 'Please,
which way did they go?' he asked the angry
woman.

She looked flustered. 'Well, I don't know,'

she said. 'I'd banged my head and I-I . . . well, I'm not entirely sure.'

With a sigh, the policeman closed his notebook.

'We'll keep our eyes peeled,' Mum promised the policeman, as Dad turned the car around.

'Are we going back?' Wendy asked hopefully, as they drove back into town.

'Yes, back on that wild goose chase,' said Dad wearily. 'Or wild ice-cream-van chase, I should say. I've a feeling it might be a long one.'

Chapter 3
The Sweet Ps

The other shops were locking up and pulling their night shutters down, but the fairy lights in the window of Sweet Ps were still lit and the **OPEN** sign still hung on the door.

'Why don't we ask in there?' suggested Wendy, but something further along the street had caught Mum's eye and she hurried past.

'You just want sweets,' said Wayne, who knew his sister.

'I don't. Well, I do,' admitted Wendy. 'But

it's that peacock till. I want to have a good
look at it.'

'You want to look at the sweets,' insisted
Wayne.

'Just keep an eye on Mum and Dad for a
minute,' pleaded Wendy.

'OK,' said Wayne. 'Hey, there's that woman

again – the one who was in the car that crashed. Mum's talking to her.'

Wendy saw the woman, further down the street, beside the bashed red car. With her hands stuck on her plump hips, she still looked angry. The rude girl who had stuck her tongue out at Wendy got out of the car – and did it again! Wendy turned her back and went into the shop.

Sweet P's smelt heavenly. Wendy stood amongst jars and jars of sweets and sniffed the sugary air.

'Can I help you, dear?'

Wendy turned around. There was no sign of anyone else. All she could see, in the gentle glow of the fairy lights that were strung all over the shop, was a puff of white candyfloss and a couple of shiny chocolates that seemed to be sitting on the counter. Wendy blinked, looked closer, and saw that it was actually a swirl of white hair above a pair of wide brown eyes. She stood on tiptoe

and realized that the hair and the eyes belonged to a tiny old lady behind the counter.

'So much choice,' said the old lady. 'Just take your time, dear.'

Wendy looked at the old-fashioned money till on the shop counter. It was *exactly* like the one inside the missing ice-cream van.

'I'd like some . . . um, some hot cinnamon gumballs,' said Wendy. Dad's old favourites were the first thing to pop into her head. 'That's a beautiful old till,' she blurted out.

'Till, dear?' The tiny old lady stopped,

paper bag in one hand, sweet scoop in the other. Wendy couldn't see how she was ever going to reach the jar of hot cinnamon gumballs on the second-highest shelf.

'Um, yes, and . . . oh, it's really strange, because *we've* got one exactly the same,' Wendy gabbled, saying the first words that popped into her head.

'One of *these*?' asked the old lady, tapping the till with her sweet scoop.

Wendy nodded. 'Well, we did. It was a metal one, all decorated in peacocks, just like yours.'

'Now, that *is* strange because, you see –' the old lady stared fondly at the till – 'Pa Periwinkle picked up this till years ago on his travels. He brought it back from . . . oh, where was it? Tansy!' she suddenly called out. 'Tansy, dear, are you there?'

'Just giving Pa his nettle and thistle tea,' a voice called from the back of the shop.

'So good for warming his old bones,' the

old lady whispered confidentially. 'Although it does tend to make him a bit of a jumping bean all evening. Now, hot cinnamon gumballs, wasn't it?'

'Yes,' said Wendy,' 'but you were going to tell me about the peacock till.'

'Ah yes,' said the old lady. 'It was so long ago and my memory is almost as shifty as Pa's these days. Tansy will remember.'

The tiny woman fetched a small set of ladders and climbed up for the hot cinnamon gumballs. She blew dust off the jar as she set it on the counter. It looked as though no one had bought cinnamon gumballs for a very long time. Then, from the back of the shop came another tiny old lady, with the same white swirl of candyfloss hair and the same brown eyes. They had to be sisters, thought Wendy.

'Now then, Dill, what is the problem?' the second old lady demanded in a brisk, bossy voice.

'Oh, there's no problem, Tansy,' said Dill.

'This young lady was just enquiring about our beautiful old till and I couldn't quite remember its story. You know how forgetful I am.'

'I most certainly do,' said Tansy. She looked at Wendy, then at the till. 'Pa picked it up *years* ago.'

'That's what I said. Oh, the things he'd bring back from his travels!' Dill clasped her hands. 'Wonderful things.'

'Not when you have to dust them every day,' said Tansy. 'All those bottles and skulls.'

Wendy gulped. *Skulls?* 'But . . . but did you ever own another peacock till?' she asked, glancing nervously around the shop for any skulls that might be lurking.

'Another till? Did we, dear?' Dill asked her sister.

'We did,' said Tansy. She looked at Wendy curiously.

'Where is it now?' asked Wendy, feeling awkward under Tansy's gaze.

'Long gone,' said Tansy. 'But why—'

'Didn't you say,' Dill interrupted, 'that *you* had one just like this?'

Wendy nodded. 'Yes. Um, you see, my mum and dad bought an ice-cream van from a scrapyard and we soon found out that she was . . . well . . . *special*. Sort of *magical*. And she had an old-fashioned till with peacocks all over it, just like this one. The thing is, she's gone missing and we're so *worried*. We love her and we can't find her.'

'Oh, dear me,' said Dill.

The two old ladies looked so concerned

that Wendy blurted out the whole story of how the ice-cream van had gone missing from the farmer's field.

'We need to find her. I don't know how you can help us, but it's just so strange to see the very same till, here in your shop. It's like finding a clue,' said Wendy.

She looked at the peacock till, half hoping it might *ching* open its money drawer and present them with a clue.

Dill grasped Tansy's hand excitedly.

Tansy looked doubtful. 'Surely that old van would only be fit for the scrap heap by now? She was in bad enough shape back then.'

'Tansy! Really! Doodle was almost human,' cried Dill.

'Doodle?' said Wendy. 'What old van? Are you . . . are you talking about . . . ?'

'*Our* ice-cream van,' said Dill. 'We called her Doodle because of her tune. *Yankee Doodle came to town*,' she sang, '*riding on a pony.*'

A smile broke across Wendy's face. '*Stuck a*

feather *in his cap and called it Macaroni.*
That's why *we* called her Macaroni!'

'Garlic gumballs!' exclaimed Dill. 'It *must*
be our old Doodle. How very extraordinary!
Tansy, we must tell Pa Periwinkle right away!'

'Wait, Dill, you know Pa mustn't get over-
excited,' warned Tansy. But she was smiling
too. 'We always wondered what became of
Doodle. One day she just disappeared.'

'That's what's happened today,' said Wendy. 'But she's somewhere around because she caused a crash just outside the town.'

'I see,' said Tansy. She gestured to Wendy to come through a gap in the counter into the back of the shop.

Before Wendy could follow, the shop door tinkled and Wayne burst in. 'Wendy! Mum and Dad are fizzing mad. They've been looking for you everywhere.'

Wendy looked guilty, then hopeful. 'Have they found Macaroni?'

Wayne shook his head. 'Nope. Mum says, how can a goat drive an ice-cream van through a town and nobody see a thing?'

He stopped, embarrassed. 'What I mean is . . .'

'Ah, because there's a big football match on TV, dear,' said Dill. 'You could probably ride a dinosaur through town right now and people wouldn't notice.'

'Wayne, just tell Mum and Dad I'm in the

sweet shop and I won't be long,' said Wendy, frowning at him.

'But you've to come right now,' said Wayne. He frowned back at his sister, wanting to know what she was up to.

'Just tell them,' said Wendy. She winked at her brother as she slipped through the gap in the counter.

Wayne looked uncertainly from Wendy to the two old ladies.

Tansy tapped Wendy's arm.

'Your brother is quite right to be

concerned, dear,' she said. 'I'm sure you've been told a thousand times not to speak to strangers.'

'But you're not really strangers if you know Macaroni,' said Wendy. 'If you once owned her then we're practically related.'

Dill's face creased into a hundred-wrinkle smile. 'Well, that's true! Tansy, we're owners-in-law.' She turned to Wayne. 'Why not fetch your parents along for a cup of tea? Then we can all put our heads together with Pa Periwinkle to see if we can find Doodle.'

'Doodle?' said Wayne.

'It's Macaroni,' explained Wendy. 'Macaroni Doodle!'

Chapter 4
Old Pa Periwinkle

Pa Periwinkle sat dozing by a crackling fire, in an armchair that was so old and squashy it looked as if it had long ago moulded to fit his wiry body. He had a single wisp of candyfloss hair that whirled up in the shape of a question mark on the crown of his head.

'Pa, we have a visitor,' said Dill.

Wide brown eyes opened in a wizened face. With his white question mark of hair, Pa Periwinkle gave the impression of an ancient but ever-curious man.

'Who is it?' asked the old man in a voice like a creaky door.

'I'm Wendy,' said Wendy, staring up at the tall, wood-framed glass cabinets that lined the walls of the cosy parlour. Bottles of every shape and size and colour filled the cabinets – almost as many bottles as there were jars of sweets in the shop, thought Wendy, wondering if they contained sweet-making ingredients. Among the bottles sat the occasional skull. Warily, Wendy peered into the nearest cabinet.

Lava Cloud Liniment read the label on a fat, scarlet bottle. Next to it was a square, blue, star-sprinkled jar of *Pimpinella Pastilles*. A small animal skull sat beside a spindly purple bottle shaped like a church steeple, containing *Cordial of Lungwort*, which sat

beside a large white tub of *Angel Balm*. Beyond these, there were teas and tinctures and tonics, oils and essences, ointments and embrocations, elixirs and lotions, bracers and balsams, and even a jar of *Dried Scorpion Tails* that made Wendy gulp.

'This is Pa Periwinkle's Apothecary,' said Tansy. 'An apothecopoeia of ancient cures and remedies. Of course, most people go to pharmacies and chemists these days.'

'Hmph,' snorted Pa.

Out front, the shop doorbell gave a violent *ting,* then the door slammed shut. 'That'll be my brother, Wayne,' said Wendy. Wayne always slammed doors.

When Dill brought Wayne through to the back parlour, he gaped as Wendy had done at the cabinets full of bottles and skulls.

'Er, Mum and Dad'll be along in a minute,' he said, his eyes fixed on a large jar of *Petrified Snake Fangs (Mixed)*.

Pa Periwinkle sat in his chair patting what

Wendy thought, at first, was the polished shell of a tortoise. With a shock, she saw that it was a skull. Pa Periwinkle talked to the skull as if it were a live person.

'Wendy and Wayne, eh, Catriona?' he said, apparently addressing the skull.

'Do you think that was his wife?' Wayne whispered to Wendy. He nodded at the skull.

'Ma Periwinkle?' said Dill, who'd

overheard. 'The skull? Ooh, what a thought.' Dill bent over and made an odd creaking noise. The children looked at the little woman in alarm, then realized she was laughing. 'No, dear, Catriona is the Manu monkey that befriended Pa when he was trying to discover the ancient magic of the Incas in the rainforests of Peru.' Still creaking with laughter, Dill pointed to the mahogany dresser stacked with plates and teacups. 'Up on the top shelf, *that's* mother up there.'

Wendy and Wayne saw a skull on the very top shelf, in between a blue-patterned pot and a daisy-covered teapot.

'In the blue Chinese pot,' said Tansy. 'Her ashes,' she added, seeing the confusion on the children's faces.

Wendy gulped. 'You were going to tell your pa about the ice-cream van.'

'Oh yes,' Dill remembered. 'Pa, you'll never believe this. These children are looking for Doodle.'

Pa Periwinkle's eyes widened in surprise, then narrowed. '*My* Doodle?'

'She's actually *our* ice-cream van,' said Wayne. 'She's called Macaroni and we've lost her.'

'*Your* ice-cream van?' said Pa. 'She is not. She's *mine*.'

'Now Pa—' began Dill.

'When did we sell her, eh, Catriona? Never. She just disappeared one night. So I say she's still mine,' said Pa Periwinkle, clutching the skull close to his chest.

'But—' said Wendy.

'We—' said Wayne.

'And when did you *buy* her, Pa?' Tansy cut in. 'Your story was that you never did. She belonged to the Californian medicine man – the one who cheated you. Maybe these two children have just as much claim to Doodle as you do.'

'He was no medicine man,' grunted Pa Periwinkle. 'He was a no-good, lying fraudster who sold me dried salamander tears that turned out to be coloured salt!'

'But he did have some kind of magic, didn't he?' said Dill. 'He put the magic powder into Doodle.'

'Magic? Him?' retorted Pa. 'It wasn't his magic. I caught him red-handed, trying to steal the Inca Fire Powder it took me months to wheedle out of the Yine tribe. He wouldn't

give it back, so we ended up fighting for it. The Fire Powder spilt all over Doodle when we were fighting. Some got into her engine and blew her bonnet off. The fraudster said a blown-up van was no use to him, so I took her as payment for his fake salamander tears. Of course, I never knew then what the Fire Powder had done to her. So you see, I did pay for her, in a way.'

'So the Fire Powder made her magic?' said Wayne.

'It surely did,' said Pa Periwinkle. A mostly toothless grin spread across his face and he patted the skull. 'Oh, Catriona, remember the adventures we had after that.'

Tansy raised her eyes to the blue Chinese pot on the top of the dresser. 'The nonsense poor mother had to put up with.'

'Your mother loved Doodle,' said Pa. 'She invented the Fizzbomb Sherbet you two used to love when you were young. Made it with the tiniest sprinkling of Fire Powder. She

spent years trying out
different recipes with
the stuff.'

'It was all those
years testing exploding
potions and powders
that probably led to
her early death,' said
Tansy.

'She *was* eighty-
seven, dear,' Dill
reminded her.

'She might have had
years left in her,' sniffed Tansy.

'Macaroni and Doodle must be the same
van, because we found a packet of Fizzbomb
Sherbet inside Macaroni – Dad made
Fizzbomb ice cream with it!' Wendy burst
out.

'*Amazing* stuff,' said Wayne, wondering if
the Periwinkles might have any more.

A bell tinkled out front in the sweet shop.

'Customers,' said Dill.

'That'll be Mum and Dad,' said Wayne, as the two old ladies bustled out to investigate.

Chapter 5
The Peripatetic
Apothecary

'A cup of nettle and ginger tea? Or would you prefer marigold?' Dill offered.

Mum and Dad sat down on a sofa that looked and felt perilously close to collapse. They stared at all the skulls and bottles.

Mum looked curiously at a bottle of *North African Sirocco Wind Bracer* on top of a pile of old books beside Pa Periwinkle's armchair. She'd been trying to smile politely at her hosts while shooting angry glares at her two children for befriending strangers and disappearing into the back of a sweet shop without permission.

'Oh, marigold tea would be lovely,' she said, guessing.

'Not for me, thank you,' said Dad, after a glance at the murky stuff that Tansy was pouring into Pa Periwinkle's teacup. 'We really should be going.'

'But, Dad, we've found a clue to the Macaroni mystery!' said Wendy.

She explained how she'd spotted the peacock till in the sweet shop, then told the story of Pa Periwinkle and the Fire Powder.

'So Macaroni really is magic, and that's why,' she finished. 'It's all because of Pa Periwinkle.'

'Fire Powder?' said Dad, looking extremely doubtful. 'Never heard of that.'

'Well, you probably wouldn't unless you were a peripathetic apocalypsy like our Pa,' said Dill.

'Say that again?' said Dad.

'Peripatetic apothecary!' exclaimed Tansy. 'Really, Dill. Will you never get it right?'

'Well, dear, as I'm seventy-two next Tuesday I'm not too sure I ever will,' giggled Dill.

'What's a peri-what's-it?' asked Wayne.

'A travelling apothecary,' said Tansy.

Dad turned to Pa Periwinkle. 'Apothecary?' he said. 'That's the old word for chemist, isn't it?'

'Chemist indeed,' snorted Pa. 'Ours is the true art, eh, Catriona?' Pa winked at the monkey skull. 'Used to travel the world, I did, searching for the lost knowledge of the ancients. Do you know what I can do with a thimbleful of vervain, a thumbnail of moon

penny, the light of a midsummer firefly and the flower of an Aztec Century Plant that blooms only once in a hundred years?'

It wasn't entirely clear if Pa was asking Dad or the skull.

'I can't imagine,' said Dad truthfully.

'Just as well,' said Pa, looking smug.

'If you're seventy-two next Tuesday,' Wendy said to Dill, daring to ask the question that had been niggling her, 'how old is Pa Periwinkle?'

Dill looked at Tansy, then at Pa, who winked and tapped the skull's nose.

'Well, he must be—'

'Oh, at least—'

'If not more—'

'Indeed.'

'He is definitely,' Tansy announced, 'quite exceedingly old.'

'Gargantuan,' agreed Dill.

'I thought that meant large,' said Wayne. 'Like a dinosaur.'

'Does it, dear? Well, Pa is almost as *old* as one,' said Dill.

Dad stood up. He looked as if he wasn't sure if he believed Pa Periwinkle's story or not. 'We really should be going. It's getting late. We'll take a last drive around to see if we can spot Macaroni, and we'll certainly let you know if there's any news.'

'And, of course, if you hear or see any sign of her . . .' Mum searched in her bag for a pen. 'Maybe we should leave our phone number.'

'Don't have a phone,' said Pa Periwinkle.

'We use the phone box on the corner,' said Dill.

'I could save you all the bother, of course,' said Pa. 'But no one thinks to ask an old man anything, do they, Catriona?'

He wriggled in his chair.

'Too much nettle and thistle tea, Pa,' muttered Tansy. 'You're jittery as a jumping bean. It's hot milk for you tonight.'

Pa made a face at Tansy. 'Bossyboots.'

Dill was eyeing the old man curiously. 'Pa,' she said, 'what *do* you mean? Ask you what? Do you know something about Doodle?'

Everyone stared at the old man.

'Pa,' said Tansy in a severe tone.

'You still haven't asked me,' said Pa stubbornly.

Wendy knelt down beside Pa.

'Please, Pa,' she said, 'do you know something about Macaroni?'

'Doodle,' insisted Pa.

'Macaroni Doodle then,' said Wendy. 'Have you seen her?'

'Oh yes,' said Pa. He winked at the monkey skull. 'Sure we have, eh, Catriona? That old van always comes back for a visit. Don't see her for ages, then one day she'll come trundling up the back lane, jingle-jangling her Yankee Doodle tune.'

'Pa! When?' gasped Dill. 'Why didn't you tell us?'

'It's our secret, eh, Catriona? A man's got

to have something that these two bossyboots don't know about.'

'Don't be silly, Pa,' said Tansy. 'You've just been dreaming in front of the fire.'

'Dreaming am I, eh, Catriona? Maybe we should all take a look outside.' Pa tucked the skull under his arm and his white question mark of hair wobbled as he pushed himself out of his chair. 'Then we'll see who's dreaming.'

Chapter 6
Nemesis of Nepenthes

Everyone trooped out of the parlour after Pa Periwinkle, through the kitchen and out of the back door. It was dark now, and the lights from the house lit up a small, narrow, brick-walled garden. A stone path led through a pleasantly messy patchwork of herb, vegetable, flower and shrub beds. They followed the old man as he click-clacked slowly down the garden path with his walking stick. Catriona was securely tucked under one arm and his white whisk of hair bobbed with each step.

He unlatched the wooden gate set into the high brick wall, and they followed him out into the back lane.

Pa Periwinkle stood and stared into the night. The windows of the street of houses that backed on to the lane threw light upon the cobblestones. Apart from a few trees and huddles of rubbish bins, the lane was empty. There was no sign whatsoever of any ice-cream van, magical or otherwise.

'Pa, dear,' said Dill. She patted his hand. 'Maybe it's those rum truffles. You do tend to gorge on them. They've been giving you funny dreams.'

'It wasn't a dream.' Pa Periwinkle clacked his stick on the cobbles. 'Doodle was here. Right *here*.'

'Well, there's nothing here now,' said Tansy firmly. 'Come on back inside, Pa.'

Pa opened his mouth as if he was going to argue. Instead there came the oddest noise. A long, muffled moan.

'I beg your pardon?' said Tansy.

'Wasn't me,' said Pa.

Bmmmmf! The noise sounded again.

It seemed to come from right behind Pa Periwinkle. Two bins had been knocked over and rubbish spilt out on to the cobbles. There

was a loud bash and a third bin crashed over
and rolled out into the lane. Another muffled
bmmmmf came from behind the rubbish bins
that were still standing.

'Stay back,' said Dad. 'May I?' He reached out for Pa's walking stick and the old man handed it to him.

'Who's there?' said Dad, brandishing the stick.

Bmmmmf! Bash! Crash!

Dad hauled away a bin. Two forlorn brown eyes stared out. Then a head poked through.

'Gina!' the children cried.

Dad lifted the remaining bins aside to let Gina out. But she couldn't move. Her feet and her mouth were bound with thick black tape.

'Oh, Gina! Who did this to you?' Mum knelt beside the frightened goat and stroked her head. 'I'm sorry, but this is going to hurt a little bit.'

Quickly, as Dad was freeing Gina's legs, Mum ripped the black tape from her mouth. Gina let out the longest, most indignant *baaaaa-aah* it was possible for a goat to make. People began to stare out of windows up and down the lane.

'I think that hurt a *lot*,' said Wayne.

'That pesky goat!' Pa Periwinkle gave a creaky cry. 'The last time Doodle came she brought that goat. Guzzled half my herb patch.'

'That's Gina,' said Wayne.

'Look at this.' Wendy, who was stroking Gina's nose to calm her, removed a note that had been paper-clipped to her left ear.

She unfolded the note and read:

I NO YUV GOT THE MAJIC POUDER AND I WUNT IT SO PUT IT RITE WHERE I LEFT THE GOTE. YUV GOT TIL MIDNITE TONITE OR I WILL SMUSH UP THE VAN AND SELL HER FOR SCRAP METIL. YUV BIN WANRED.

Wendy frowned. 'I think that should be *warned*.'

Pa Periwinkle took the note from Wendy and studied it.

'Swindling quacksalver! Horn-swoggling cheat!' he erupted, his face scarlet with outrage. 'Bamboozling trickster!'

'And a rotten speller,' added Wendy.

'Pa, dear,' cried Dill. 'Do calm down. You must not let him upset you.'

'I'm not upset. I'm fizzbombing furious!'

'You know who wrote this?' said Dad.

Pa stamped his walking stick on the cobbles. 'I know gimcracker bunkum when I see it.'

'Who *is* it?' asked Dad.

The three Periwinkles looked at each other.

'It's a long story,' said Tansy.

'It's Mugwort,' sighed Dill. 'Pa's nephew. His brother's son. Such a nice child he was, once.'

'No, he wasn't,' snapped Tansy. 'He was always a nasty little thief. He used to steal sweets, then put stones in the jars in their place. And his spelling is so terrible because no school would ever keep him.'

'True, dear,' remembered Dill.

'That flapdoodling young rogue's no relation of ours any more. I disowned him years ago,' cried Pa Periwinkle. 'He's been after Doodle and her magic for as long as I can remember. If I ever catch him I'll empty a canister of cankerworm over him!'

'What'll that do?' asked Wayne.

'Canker him from head to toe,' grunted Pa, 'and serve him right.'

'Think of a human volcano, dear,' said Dill, shuddering. 'A mass of erupting boils – Not a pretty sight. Now, let's take this poor goat indoors. A sip of chamomile might calm her.'

'But we need to find Macaroni Doodle,' said Wendy. 'We can't let this Mugwort smush . . . I mean, smash her up for scrap metal.'

'Of course we can't,' said Mum.

'I'll call the police,' said Dad. He began to search his pockets for his phone.

'I wouldn't do that,' said Pa Periwinkle.

'Neither would I,' said Mum.

Back in the parlour, while Dill made Gina some calming chamomile tea, Pa gazed around at the shelves of apothecary bottles.

'Hmm,' he grunted every so often. 'Aha. What do you think, eh, Catriona?' He consulted the skull.

At last he sank into his chair and gave Catriona a quick hug. 'Excellent idea.'

While Wayne tried to get Gina to sit still and Wendy tried to get her to drink chamomile tea from a yellow china cup, Dad finally found his mobile phone – in Mum's bag – but before he could call the police, Mum grabbed his hand.

'The old man seems to know all about this

Mugwort,' she whispered. 'Let's hear his idea first. The police might have a lot of questions about Macaroni after that accident she caused today.' Mum paused. 'Anyway, what would we say to them – that our runaway magical ice-cream van caused an accident, then was stolen by some rogue who left a ransom note on our goat because he's after the magic powder an old peripatetic apothecary once got from a tribe in Peru? Do you think the police are going to swallow a tale like that? It could all get very *difficult*.'

Dad put his phone in his pocket.

'What are you up to, Pa?' said Tansy.

The old man was waving his walking stick in the air.

'Ladders, Tansy, the ladders.'

'Now, Pa, remember what happened the last time you went up.' Dill turned to Mum. 'He took a dizzy turn. We had to fetch the window cleaner from along the road to get him down again.'

'Oh dear,' said Mum.

'This young man –' Pa Periwinkle pointed his walking stick at Dad – 'could go up and fetch it for me.'

'Certainly,' said Dad, looking pleased at being called a young man.

Pa Periwinkle pointed to a set of small step-ladders leaning against the wall behind his saggy armchair.

'Well, Pa, what can I get you?' Dad lifted out the ladders.

Pa pointed up at the cabinet beside the fire. 'Top shelf, small amethyst bottle.'

Tansy and Dill gasped.

'What is it?' asked Dad. One foot on the ladder, he paused.

'Nemesis of Nepenthes,' said Pa Periwinkle. His eyes gleamed.

'Is it poison?' asked Wayne.

'Oh dear, no,' said Dill indignantly. 'Pa doesn't deal in poisons.'

Wayne looked disappointed.

Dad climbed up and found the small amethyst bottle. Once back on the ground, he peered at the purple contents, then took the stopper in his forefinger and thumb, curious to see what was inside.

'No!' cried Dill and Tansy.

Dad froze.

'I wouldn't do that,' Pa chuckled as Dad handed him the bottle. 'Never mess with Nemesis of Nepenthes, my boy.'

The old man sat the little bottle on the arm of his chair, beside Catriona. It looked as if the skull were watching over it. Pa Periwinkle winked at Catriona and leaned forward in his chair. His whisk of hair quivered and his voice was as creaky as an old door in the wind. 'I'm not called Periwinkle for nothing. The periwinkle is the hardiest of herbs.'

Tansy coughed. 'Just remember, Pa, Mugwort's a Periwinkle too. He's hard in his own horrible way.'

'Mugwort,' said Pa, 'is a much lesser Periwinkle. Just like that brother of mine was, I'm afraid. Now listen. Here's what we'll do.'

Chapter 7
The Lesser Periwinkle

Mugwort Periwinkle sat in the back of the ice-cream van, mixing up a tincture that he had found in *Apothecary for Beginners*, a book he'd stolen long ago from Pa Periwinkle. It was the only recipe he had ever managed to learn. The book was mostly too hard for him to read.

In a small brown bottle he put a pinch of Mimulus to stop him being scared. A large pinch of Rock Rose would stop any awkward nerves and a smidgen of Red Chestnut would calm sudden worries. He also tipped in a good measure of Powdered Elm extract to keep his wits about him. They tended to abandon him when he was about to do something *really* bad.

A lifetime spent doing lots of bad things had made Mugwort a nervous man. He had gulped down so much Red Chestnut and Powdered Elm over the years that he'd probably swallowed a small forest. He thought it was bad to be scared of doing bad things. Never once had he thought that it might be a good idea to listen to his fear and stop all the lying, stealing, robbing and thieving.

Mugwort tipped in a bit more Elm, just for

luck, because tonight's robbery would be the steal of his life.

For years, Mugwort had tried and failed to get his hands on Pa Periwinkle's magic Fire Powder. Many times he had tried to steal the ice-cream van, but the van seemed to know what he was up to, because she always locked her doors tight shut when he was around. It was the goat who had finally given him his chance. Mugwort had been hanging round in the back lane, looking through the Periwinkles' rubbish bins, as he used to do with his father, hopeful that he might find something he shouldn't.

Mugwort couldn't believe it when the ice-cream van had come jingle-jangling up the lane. He hadn't seen her in years, though he'd always kept an eye out for her. The van never knew he was there, crouched among the bins, and when she'd swung her doors open to let the goat out, Mugwort had taken his chance and jumped into the driver's seat.

Luckily, he always carried a roll of strong masking tape in his pocket. You never knew the minute you might get the chance to rob, so it was always a good idea to have some tape at the ready to bind and gag anyone who got in your way.

Ever since, as a boy, his father had told him the secret of the ice-cream van's magic, Mugwort had longed to get hold of the Fire Powder. His father, Wort, had been after it too and made many failed attempts to get his hands on it. It was his dying wish that his son, Mugwort, would one day, as he said, get *his* thieving hands on it.

Wort had turned bad through jealousy. Mugwort knew his father thought of himself as a lesser Periwinkle – always in the shadow of his older brother, the famous apothecary, who boasted to Wort that he had discovered the secrets of the ancient apothecaries on his travels across the world. Wort had passed his badness and jealousy on to Mugwort. And tonight, at midnight, Mugwort was finally about to fulfil his father's dying wish and get his thieving hands on one of those ancient secrets. He would have the Fire Powder at last. No longer would he be a lesser Periwinkle. He would be a greater Periwinkle. The greatest Periwinkle of all!

Mugwort put the cork stopper in the small glass bottle and shook the tincture. He took the stopper out, held his nose (it smelt like dead mice and tasted like venom) and got ready to take a gulp. Just one – it was potent stuff. But at the very moment he put the bottle to his lips, the ice-cream van gave a violent shudder, as if a giant hand was shaking her from side to side. Mugwort choked as most of the tincture glugged down his throat.

Dazed, he waited for a second to see what would happen. His insides felt a bit fiery, his head throbbed and he burped loudly, but nothing else happened. Mugwort kicked the wall of the ice-cream van.

'Just behave, you!' he told her. 'Or I'll put hot chilli powder in your engine and stinging-nettle juice in your petrol tank and see how you like that. Then I'll take you to the scrapyard and get them to crush you as flat as an envelope. You hear?'

Macaroni let out an angry jangle, then fell still and quiet.

Mugwort looked at his watch. Nearly time to go. He slipped into the driver's seat and gripped the steering wheel.

'Right, no nonsense, you,' he told the van, 'or else. Get going. Make it snappy.'

Macaroni's engine rumbled. Then she accelerated so hard down the dusty forest path they'd been hiding in that Mugwort bashed his head on the window.

'Whoa, there!' he yelled as they bounced and rattled over the rough, bumpy track. The tincture glugged in his stomach, making him feel sick rather than brave.

Macaroni's tyres screeched to a halt. Mugwort clenched his jaw and gritted his teeth. He peered into the darkness as he turned the van on to the main road that led to the seaside town where Pa Periwinkle lived – and where the magic powder awaited him.

Chapter 8
Nemesis of Gina

At the very moment Mugwort was steering Macaroni on to the main road, Wendy and Wayne, Mum, Dill, Tansy and Pa were all gathered expectantly in the Periwinkles' parlour. They had each rubbed their faces with soot from the fireplace to camouflage themselves in the dark.

'Let's just hope it doesn't rain,' said Mum.

'Now, does everyone understand the plan?' asked Pa.

Five sooty faces nodded back at him.

Another sooty person entered the kitchen from the back garden.

'All set?' said Dad, stepping into the parlour. 'I've put the bottle of Nemesis of

Nepenthes behind the bins, right where we found Gina.'

'Did you see anyone in the lane?' asked Wendy anxiously.

'Not a sausage,' said Dad.

'That boy's such a flapdoodler I wouldn't be surprised if he got the wrong night,' said Pa.

'Are you sure about doing this nemesis thing if he's just a boy?' said Mum.

'That "boy" must be sixty if he's a day,' said Tansy.

'You still haven't told us exactly what Nemesis of Nepenthes does,' said Wayne.

'One whiff of Nepenthes,' said Pa, 'makes you instantly forget whatever it is you long for.' Pa winked confidentially at Catriona, who was tucked under his arm. The monkey skull had been blacked with soot too.

'Nemesis,' said Mum thoughtfully. 'Doesn't that mean getting the punishment you deserve?'

'That's Nemesis.' Pa's sooty face creased

with a wicked smile. 'And Mugwort's nemesis is long overdue.'

What will Mugwort's nemesis be? Wendy wondered. But she would have to wait to find out what punishment *he* deserved.

'Time to get going. It's ten minutes to midnight,' warned Tansy.

They crept outside, down the garden path and into the lane, where they had planned a hiding place behind a tree and a neighbour's rubbish bins. In the darkness of the lane, their sooty faces made them almost invisible. All except for –

'Your hair!' Wayne hissed.

Somehow, no one had given it a thought, but the white swirls of hair that rose from the heads of the Periwinkles seemed to float in the dark like three tiny ghosts.

'Spooky,' giggled Wendy.

'Too late now,' said Dad. 'Just keep your heads down.'

As he spoke, there came a noise that made

the children want to jump with joy. It was the
sound of Macaroni trundling up the cobbled
lane, with a sad, low jingle-jangle tune.

'Shurrup, you!' they heard a voice threaten.
'Or you'll be scrap by tomorrow lunchtime.
I've warned you.'

Wendy squeaked indignantly. Wayne put his hand over her mouth.

'He'll get what's coming to him,' muttered Pa.

Mugwort got out of the van. Macaroni's headlights showed a small, wiry man with a Periwinkle tuft of hair rush over to the rubbish bins on the opposite side of the lane, where he had left Gina bound and gagged. They heard him scrabbling frantically among the bins. When he found what he thought he was looking for he gave a gleeful chuckle that would make a pantomime villain proud.

Mugwort lifted the bottle of Nemesis of Nepenthes to look at it in the blaze of the ice-cream van's headlights. The little amethyst bottle glowed.

'He won't be able to resist,' murmured Pa.

And Mugwort couldn't. He pulled the stopper from the bottle and peered inside at the Nemesis of Nepenthes.

'Just a sniff,' Pa whispered.

Mugwort put the little amethyst bottle to his nose and sniffed. And sniffed again. A dreamy vagueness began to soften his bitter face. He looked around him and at the ice-cream van, as if he couldn't quite remember where he was or why he was there. Then he looked as if he really couldn't care. He sat down on the cobbles, leaned against the bins, and glugged down the Nemesis of Nepenthes.

'Have you got the bag of Fizzbomb, Tansy?' said Pa.

'Right here, Pa,' said Tansy, and she handed him a large paper bag.

'Now that the Nepenthes has made him forget what grieves him,' whispered Pa, 'his nemesis is that he'll believe that this bag of Fizzbomb Sherbet is the Fire Powder.' He winked. 'There's never been sherbet quite like this one. I've made it extra strong.'

'Pa, you're a genie,' said Dill.

'Genius,' corrected Tansy.

'I know what I meant, bossyboots,' said Dill. 'Pa's so clever he'll make all our wishes come true.'

'Girls!' hissed Pa. 'Someone help me up.'

Crouching behind the bins in the cold night air had made Pa's old bones freeze up. With Tansy and Dill on each side and Mum and Dad pushing from behind, Pa Periwinkle was brought to a standing position and he walked into the light of the ice-cream van's headlights.

'Mugwort, my lad!' cried Pa as if he was delighted to see his long-lost nephew. 'I got your note. There's no need for us to quarrel. You're my one and only nephew, my brother's son, and I *want* you to inherit my secret. The magic powder is all yours, Mugwort.' Pa's eyes gleamed.

Mugwort stared at Pa, then chuckled. 'Pa, your face is all sooty.'

'I've been emptying the coal scuttle,' said Pa. 'But never mind that, Mugwort. Don't you want my magic powder? Isn't that what you came for?'

Pa held up the large bag of Fizzbomb Sherbet.

Mugwort looked vague. He frowned, as if trying to remember what he had come for. Then, as he looked at the bag, he seemed to remember.

'Yes!' Mugwort bounded to his feet. 'The magic powder!'

He grabbed the bag from Pa, grinning.

At this, Macaroni, who had begun to jingle anxiously, let out a loud blare of her horn. She began to jangle furiously and shake from side to side.

'Macaroni, shhhh!'

'It's all right.'

Wendy and Wayne ran out from their hiding place and tried to calm Macaroni, who thought that Pa really was handing over his magic powder to a man she knew was a rogue. But the ice-cream van could not be calmed. She only blared her horn louder and longer.

Lights snapped on in neighbouring houses. Then a shriek filled the lane.

'Jasper! It's that van. It's in our back lane. Call the police at once!'

It was the angry woman from the bashed red car. The car that Macaroni and Gina had caused to crash. The woman marched up the lane wearing pink pyjamas.

She looks like a giant pink marshmallow, thought Wayne.

'Is she your neighbour?' Wendy asked Dill and Tansy.

'Unfortunately,' muttered Tansy. 'Mrs Snark,' she called to the woman, 'I'm so sorry for the disturb—'

'*What* are you Periwinkles *doing*, waking up the entire street in the middle of the night?' Mrs Snark demanded. Her daughter, in pink pyjamas too, crept up the lane behind her mother.

'You know, there isn't enough chamomile tea in the world to calm that woman,' sighed Dill.

The grown-ups tried to apologize, but Mrs Snark swept aside their attempts.

'Is this *your* van?' she asked Pa. 'The van that nearly killed me and my family yesterday afternoon? It was speeding like a maniac! And that –' she pointed behind Pa, outraged. '– that goat was the driver!'

Everyone looked. Gina the goat stood in the lane. The chewed-off end of the rope that was supposed to be keeping her tied up in the garden dangled from her neck.

'I'll have that animal put down,' the woman threatened.

Macaroni gave a furious blast of her horn. She flung her driver's door open and it whacked Mrs Snark hard on the bottom. At that very moment Gina, who had recognized Mugwort as the rogue who had bound and gagged her and then kidnapped Macaroni, charged.

Mugwort didn't have time to move before Gina butted him in the stomach. The bag of

Fizzbomb flew out of his hands and scattered
all over Mrs Snark and her daughter, who was
standing right behind.

Mrs Snark gave an enormous shriek. The daughter let out a wail.

'Mummy! It's in my eyes.'

The girl put her hands up to her face and as she did so sweets scattered from her pyjama top. In the pandemonium, she had sneaked into the ice-cream van for a quick snoop. Wendy and Wayne knew she must

have found Macaroni's secret hoard of never-ending sweets. The twins could scoff these sweets as much as they liked – Macaroni always magicked up more.

'I'll sue the lot of you if my child has been blinded!' the woman screeched. 'And . . . and I'll put that horrible goat down myself.'

She glared at Gina, who had settled down to munch the sweets, wrappers and all, that had scattered on the ground. But Macaroni gave out such a furious *jangle!* that the woman and her daughter clutched each other in fright.

'Just one thing left to do,' said Pa. He winked at Dad. 'Young man, would you do the honours?'

'Certainly, Pa.'

The strong black masking tape that Mugwort always carried in his pockets (in case there was ever an occasion that required someone to be bound and gagged) had fallen out of his pocket. While Mum, the two children, Tansy and Dill held on to Mugwort,

Dad bound and gagged him. Then they tipped the lesser Periwinkle into a rubbish bin to await the police.

'Just where he belongs,' said Pa.

Chapter 9
Nemesis of Fizzbombs

'The police are on their way,' said Tansy. 'Your mum and dad are going to wait with Mugwort until they're here.'

'May I offer you a good, strong cup of chamomile tea?' Dill asked Mrs Snark, who had insisted on coming into the Periwinkles' house to wait for the police.

'Very kind,' sniffed Mrs Snark, who was covered from head to foot in yellow Fizzbomb Sherbet. She sneezed for the umpteenth time. 'But first I'd like to visit the smallest room in the house.'

Dill looked puzzled. 'Which *is* our smallest room, dear?' she asked Tansy. 'The broom cupboard?'

'The cloakroom toilet,' said Tansy. 'I think Mrs Snark would like to wash up.'

'Oh, of course,' said Dill, taking a step backwards to avoid the yellow powder cloud that engulfed Mrs Snark and daughter. 'Last door on your left.'

'I wouldn't do that,' muttered Pa Periwinkle as they left the room.

'Do what?' asked Wayne.

'Wouldn't put water near extra-strong Fizzbomb. Eh, Catriona?' said Pa, stroking the monkey skull.

Wendy and Wayne looked interested.

'Anything wet sets it off,' said Pa. 'It'll stay nice and quiet in a sherbet wrapper or a sealed tin but as soon as you lick it, or add the tiniest drop of liquid or moisture . . .' Pa sucked a breath through his mostly toothless gums.

FIZZZZZZZ!

'. . . like water or even a damp cloth . . .' said Pa, a gleam in his eye.

Fizzz! ZIP! ZAP! ZOP!

'Or ice-cream?' said Wayne, remembering the Fizzbomb ice-cream they had once, accidentally, invented.

'. . . that's what happens.' Pa gave a mostly toothless grin as a crescendo of fizzbombs erupted.

POP! POW! ZAP!

'Mummy!'

FIZZZZ! BIP-PIP-PIP-POP!

'EEEEEYEEEK!'

'Never heard it do that before,' said Pa. He winked at the children.

'What on *earth* is that?' Tansy burst into the room. There was no sense to be had from the children or Dill, who were in fits of laughter, or from Pa, who had a laugh that

sounded like worn-out bagpipes. But as the
explosions in the toilet continued, Tansy
realized what had happened and couldn't help
but join in.

'We'd better get them out,' she eventually said reluctantly. 'After all, there is a child to consider.'

'A horrible one,' said Wendy.

'Indeed,' said Dill, wiping her eyes. 'But I suppose we should. In a moment or two . . .'

At Tansy and Dill's urging, Mrs Snark and the girl stopped trying to wash off the Fizzbomb Sherbet and eventually emerged in the parlour doorway. They were almost unrecognizable. Now, not only were they yellow from head to toe, their hair stood on end and their once-pink pyjamas were in tatters. They looked as if they'd been dragged through at least four hedges backwards, then endured a severe blasting from gale-force winds.

'A couple of exploded canaries,' wheezed Pa Periwinkle.

'Totally fizzbombed,' laughed Wayne.

Mrs Snark sank on to the saggy sofa. The occasional fizz, pop and zap still erupted from her person.

'You could always have a shower, dear,' offered Dill. 'The experience might be a bit violent, but you'd get it over with all at once.'

'Or my girls could give you a good shake and beating, like they do to get dust out of the rugs,' said Pa. 'Tansy, where's the carpet beater?'

'Don't you dare!' Mrs Snark struggled out of the sagging couch. 'I've had quite enough violence for one night. Maniac goats and vans and . . . and now my darling child and I have been turned into human fireworks. Come along, my pet. Mummy will rescue you from all this. We shall speak to the police.'

'I'm sure the police would like to know your pet is a little thief,' said Tansy. 'We all saw those sweets she stole from the van. You really wouldn't want that in the local paper, would you, Mrs Snark?'

The woman opened her mouth as if she might give one of her enormous shrieks. Wayne and Wendy covered their ears just in case. But she only took her daughter by the hand and marched from the parlour, out of the back door.

'I wouldn't do that,' said Pa Periwinkle.

'Do what?' said Wayne.

'Listen,' said Pa. With his walking stick he pointed to the window where rain had begun to slash against the glass pane. 'Wouldn't go out in the rain, would you, eh, Catriona?' Pa tutted at the skull. 'Not covered in Fizzbomb.'

Wayne spluttered. The widest grin spread across Wendy's face.

'Upstairs!' said Dill.

Dill raced out of the parlour and into the hall. Tansy and the children followed her upstairs to a back bedroom. Out in the lane, the darkness was lit up by flashes and sparks. The downpour of rain had set off more fizzbombs in the yellow powder that clung to the clothes of Mrs Snark and her daughter. The explosions were even more

spectacular than the ones that had taken place in the Periwinkles' toilet.

And from the rubbish bins came another burst of sparks and flashes as the rain set off the Fizzbomb Sherbet that had spilled over Mugwort.

WHEE! FIZZZZZ! POP-POP-POP-POP-ZZZZIP! went the fizzbombs as Jasper Snark ran out of their house, two doors down, to help.

'Eleanor, darling, *do* try to keep calm,' he entreated, as he tried to extinguish the fizzbombs with his bare hands.

ZAP! PIP-PIP-PIP! POP!

'Calm!' shrieked Eleanor. 'How can I keep calm when I'm exploding? Stop *thumping* me, Jasper.'

'Sorry, dear, I'm just trying to—'

PIZZZZ-OP! FIZZZZZZzzzzzzZAP! PAP-PAP-POP!

With a lot of patting and cajoling and, in the end, some hard shoving, Jasper managed to get his fizzbombed wife and daughter up their garden path and into the house. But Wendy and Wayne had seen, by the flickering flashes of fizzbombs and the house lights, that Jasper had been struggling to control a fit of laughter.

'Poor man. They must be a nightmare to live with, those two,' said Wendy.

'Yes, dear.' Dill smiled. 'But people do sometimes get what they deserve. And I think Mrs Snark just did, didn't she?'

'Nemesis of Fizzbombs,' agreed Wayne.

Chapter 10
The Periwinkle Plan

Mugwort didn't go quietly with the police. The fizzbomb explosions made sure of that.

Mum and Dad, without telling a lie, but not quite telling *all* of the truth, told the police he had stolen the ice-cream van. Somehow, the police went away with the idea that Mugwort was driving the van when it caused the crash outside town the previous day.

'What'll happen to Mugwort?' asked Wendy. 'He doesn't seem to remember a thing.'

'He can't, thanks to the Nepenthes,' said Pa. 'It's wiped the whole episode from his mind. So there's no way the police can find out about the Fire Powder. They'll probably charge him with stealing the van and dangerous driving. And that's just the nemesis he deserves, eh, Catriona? I'm sure there'll be more nonsense from Mugwort, but at least he's been scared off my magic Fire Powder. He's a scaredy-cat at the best of times, that one.'

'It's a fascinating art,' said Mum, gazing around the parlour at all the apothecary bottles. 'How exactly do you get to be an apothecary, Pa?'

The twins and their father stared at her in horror.

'I really don't think this is a good idea,' said Dad nervously.

Pa Periwinkle settled back in his chair with a wistful look on his face.

'First,' he said, 'you must leave your family

and all that you know and travel to the unknown places of the world to search out the secrets of the ancients. You'll have to brave sandstorms, landslides, erupting volcanoes, venomous snakes and spiders in

the deepest jungles, ferocious tribes, dangerous animals, frostbite and blizzards, the most terrible thirst in buring hot deserts, and lots of hunger everywhere else. It takes years and years. And that's just your apprenticeship.' The old man pointed to a book that sat on a low shelf among his apothecary bottles. The book was as wide as Pa himself. 'After that, you begin to learn all that's in *The Apothecopoeia*. That takes many more years. Only then can you begin to practise as an apothecary.'

'That's why,' said Dill, 'they're all so *very* old.'

'I see,' said Mum. She looked stunned. 'In that case, I might prefer to try something else.'

Wendy and Wayne waited.

'Let me think,' said Mum, taking a fourth rum truffle from a bowl that Tansy was handing round to warm everyone up. 'These are delicious.'

The children exchanged glances with the Periwinkles.

'Maybe Macaroni Doodle is fed up with a quiet life in a farmer's field,' said Wendy.

'Maybe she just needed a rest after her last lot of adventures,' said Wayne.

'Maybe she's ready for some more now,' added Wendy.

'From time to time the magic does tire out,' said Pa. 'But in my experience, it always restores itself after a rest. Doodle needs rest *and* adventure.'

'There's a practical solution, of course,' said Tansy, winking at the children. 'Leave Macaroni Doodle as company for Pa during the week, then at weekends you can all take her out to sell our sweets and ice-cream on the sea front. She used to love that. Pa's too old now, and Dill and I are too busy with the shop.'

'Tansy, dear,' cried Dill. 'That's a truly wonderful idea.'

'The best!' said Wendy.

Mum and Dad looked at each other.

'Ice-cream *was* our most successful business ever,' admitted Mum.

'Painting and decorating has its downside,' confessed Dad, who had hung an entire room of wallpaper upside down last week.

'Let's ask Macaroni Doodle,' suggested Wayne. 'I bet she says yes.'

'As long as you control that goat,' warned Pa. 'I'm not having my herb garden munched up every week.'

'Where *is* Gina?' asked Dad.

'Haven't seen her in a while,' said Wayne.

'She must still be in the back lane with Macaroni Doodle,' said Mum, hoping the goat *hadn't* munched up Pa's herb garden again.

They went out into the lane. It lay in darkness. Then Macaroni Doodle switched on her lights.

'Listen,' said Wendy.

'What's that?'.

'That,' said Dill, 'sounds like someone being horribly sick.'

'That's the sound of a *goat* being horribly sick,' said Wayne.

'A greedy goat who's made herself sick on sweets,' said Wendy, pointing to the evidence on the ground.

'And sweet wrappers,' added Dad.

'And the contents of quite a few rubbish bins,' said Mum, looking around. 'Will that goat never learn?'

'As long as she's left my herb garden alone,' said Pa Periwinkle.

Gina emerged from the rubbish bins looking as sick as a goat could. The ice-cream van gave a sympathetic beep of her horn.

'Let's tell Macaroni Doodle what we've planned,' said Wayne.

'Before I do, I want her to promise to behave,' warned Mum. 'You really can't go rampaging around the streets,' she told the ice-cream van, 'or you might cause a nasty accident one day.'

Macaroni Doodle gave a guilty jangle.

'But *if* you promise to behave, here's what we'll do.' Mum explained the Periwinkle plan.

Macaroni Doodle flashed her headlights. She let out a loud blast of her horn. There was a rustling noise from somewhere deep inside her, then a mechanical-sounding cough and a couple of hiccups. Finally, with a great WHOOSH, a shower of sweets burst from the horn on the ice-cream van's roof.

'I think that's a *yes*, eh, Catriona?' said Pa Periwinkle, with a mostly toothless grin.

by Julie Bertagna

Have you read the first, deliciously exciting
THE ICE-CREAM MACHINE adventure?
Find out what happened when the
Potts twins first met Macaroni!

Marshmallow Squidge, Stingy Strawberry,
Chocwobble, Cheesy Peasmint – the Potts
family sells the craziest ice cream ever!
Wayne and Wendy's parents love coming up
with weird ways to make money. But something
usually goes wrong! This time they've bought
an ice-cream van called Macaroni. When some
Fizzbomb Sherbet gets mixed in with the ice
cream, there's chaos! The family's very naughty
pet goat, Gina, is in the middle of the trouble.
And so is Macaroni, who might just be a
magical ice-cream van . . .

Gwyneth Rees

Cosmo
and the
Magic Sneeze

'A-A-A-TISHOO!' Cosmo burst out, sending a huge
shower of magic sneeze into the cauldron.

Cosmo has always wanted to be a witch-cat, just like his
father, so when he passes the special test he's really
excited. He can't wait to use his magic sneeze to help Sybil
the witch mix her spells.

Sybil is very scary, with her green belly button and toe-
nails, and no one trusts her. So when she starts brewing a
secret spell recipe – and advertising for kittens – Cosmo
and his friend Scarlett begin to worry. Could Sybil be
cooking up a truly terrifying spell? And could the extra-
special ingredient be KITTENS?

A purrfectly funny and spooky story starring one brave
kitten who finds himself in a cauldronful of trouble.

A selected list of titles available from Macmillan Children's Books

The prices shown below are correct at the time of going to press.
However, Macmillan Publishers reserves the right to show new retail prices
on covers, which may differ from those previously advertised.

JULIE BERTAGNA

| The Ice-Cream Machine | ISBN-13: 978-0-330-43746-2 | £3.99 |
| | ISBN-10: 0-330-43746-1 | |

GWYNETH REES

Mermaid Magic	ISBN-13: 978-0-330-042632-9	£4.99
	ISBN-10: 0-330-42632-X	
Fairy Dust	ISBN-13: 978-0-330-41554-5	£4.99
	ISBN-10: 0-330-41554-9	
Fairy Treasure	ISBN-13: 978-0-330-43730-1	£4.99
	ISBN-10: 0-330-43730-5	
Fairy Dreams	ISBN-13: 978-0-330-43476-8	£4.99
	ISBN-10: 0-330-43476-4	
Fairy Gold	ISBN-13: 978-0-330-43938-1	£4.99
	ISBN-10: 0-330-43938-3	
Cosmo and the Magic Sneeze	ISBN-13: 978-0-330-43729-5	£4.99
	ISBN-10: 0-330-43729-1	
Cosmo and the Great Witch Escape	ISBN-13: 978-0-330-43733-2	£4.99
	ISBN-10: 0-330-43733-X	

All Pan Macmillan titles can be ordered from our website,
www.panmacmillan.com, or from your local bookshop
and are also available by post from:

Bookpost, PO Box 29, Douglas, Isle of Man IM99 1BQ
Credit cards accepted. For details:
Telephone: 01624 677237
Fax: 01624 670923
Email: bookshop@enterprise.net
www.bookpost.co.uk

Free postage and packing in the United Kingdom